SWAN LAKE

ADAPTED AND ILLUSTRATED BY

RACHEL ISADORA

G. P. PUTNAM'S SONS • NEW YORK

G. P. Putnam's Sons, a division of The Putnam & Grosset
Book Group, 200 Madison Avenue, New York, NY 10016.
Published simultaneously in Canada.
Printed in Hong Kong by South China Printing Co. (1988) Ltd.
Book design by Nanette Stevenson
The text is set in Cochin.
Calligraphy by Jeanyee Wong

Library of Congress Cataloging-in-Publication Data
Isadora, Rachel.
Swan Lake: a ballet story / by Rachel Isadora.
p.   cm.
An adaptation of the story of Tchaikovsky's ballet.
Summary: A prince's love for a swan queen overcomes an evil
sorcerer's spell in this fairy tale adaptation of the classic ballet.
[1. Ballets—Stories, plots, etc. 2. Fairy tales.]
I. Tchaikovsky, Peter Ilich, 1840-1893. Lebedinoe ozero.
II. Title.   PZ8.I84Sw 1989   [E]—dc19   88-29843 CIP AC
ISBN 0-399-21730-4
3   5   7   9   10   8   6   4   2

For Gillian and Nicholas

Once upon a time, a widowed queen and her son, Siegfried, lived in a palace on the edge of the forest.

It was the eve of the Prince's twenty-first birthday. The Queen went to find her son, who was celebrating in the palace gardens with his friends.

"Tomorrow is your birthday ball," the Queen reminded Siegfried. "Now that you have come of age, you must choose a bride from among the royal guests." Leaving him no choice in the matter, the Queen returned to the palace.

But there is no one I love, thought Siegfried.

Just then one of the young men pointed toward the evening sky.

"Look there!" he cried. "A flock of wild swans. Let's
give them chase."

Quickly Siegfried and his friends gathered their
crossbows and arrows, mounted their horses, and set off.
In the excitement of the hunt, Siegfried forgot about the
ball and his mother's wishes.

They rode deep into the forest until it was too dark for them to see their way. Tired and discouraged, the young men turned back. Only Siegfried, eager to find the wild swans, went on alone. The forest had become so thick with tangled vines and branches that he had to lead his horse on foot.

At last he came to a clearing beside a lake. Shadows appeared on the lake's surface. The whirring of swans' wings in the sky above broke the silence. Siegfried hid and watched the swans land on the water. One by one, they glided past him, led by a swan wearing a glittering crown.

As they came up onto the shore, Siegfried readied his crossbow and took aim. Before he released an arrow, the swans turned into young maidens.

Amazed, Siegfried stepped from his hiding place. The silver-crowned maiden came toward him. When she saw the crossbow, she drew back, frightened.

"Do not be afraid," Siegfried said. "I will not harm you."

She stepped closer. Siegfried had never seen anyone as beautiful or as sad as this swan maiden.

"Who are you?" he whispered.

"I am Odette, Queen of the Swans. Long ago the evil sorcerer Von Rothbart turned my handmaidens and me into swans.

"The spell will be broken when I find a prince who will take me as his bride and pledge his love to me forever. Until then, we live as wild swans by day and ourselves by night."

Siegfried was so moved by Odette's story that he reached out to take her hand. Suddenly, a terrible screeching and flapping of wings sounded overhead. The water churned and swirled. A monstrous owl swooped down over the lake toward him.

"Von Rothbart!" Odette cried. Siegfried raised his crossbow. "No," she said, "that will not harm him." The giant owl swept low over their heads once more and flew off into the mist and darkness.

Siegfried held a trembling Odette in his arms. "I love you," he whispered. Then he told her about the ball. "Come to the palace tomorrow at nightfall. I will declare my love for you before all the court and ask you to be my bride."

They talked through the night until the first glow of dawn. Siegfried looked out over the lake and watched a flock of swans gliding by. When he turned back to Odette, she was no longer there. The Queen of the Swans had returned to her friends.

The next evening at the ball, Siegfried watched for the sun to go down so that Odette could appear as the beautiful maiden he saw at the lake.

As he waited, trumpets sounded and the ballroom doors swung open. A splendid nobleman with a beard as red as fire entered. This was the sorcerer Von Rothbart. With him was his daughter, Odile, whom he had transformed into the likeness of Odette.

Siegfried was so blinded by her beauty he did not see that the feathers she wore were now black. He swept her into his arms to dance.

Odette flew to the palace just before dark. Through the window, she saw Siegfried dancing with Odile. She beat her wings to warn him.

But he saw only Odile. "I love you," he told her, "and I will be faithful to you forevermore." A crash of thunder sounded, and lightning lit up the sky. Only then did Siegfried see the frightened swan and realize that he had broken his promise to Odette.

He heard Von Rothbart's laughter fill the ballroom. "I have lost Odette!" he cried out in despair.

Siegfried ran from the palace. When he reached the clearing beside the lake, he found Odette lying on the ground. He lifted her gently. "Will you forgive me?" he whispered.

As he held her, a shadow passed across the moon. Out of the darkness, the giant owl appeared. It flew at Siegfried with sharp talons extended.

"No!" Siegfried cried, and rushed at the owl. His love for Odette gave him strength. He struck the owl, and the great bird fell to the ground with a terrifying screech. Siegfried looked down and saw that he had killed the sorcerer Von Rothbart.

The maidens gathered round. "You have released us from the spell," they said joyously. Siegfried and Odette embraced.

"We will never be apart again," Siegfried told Odette, as the first light of dawn shimmered across Swan Lake.